Bird & Birdie

in

A Fine Day

ETHAN LONG

TRICYCLE PRESS

Berkeley

Text and illustrations copyright © 2010
by Ethan Long

All rights reserved.
Published in the United States by
Tricycle Press, an imprint of the Crown
Publishing Group, a division of Random
House, Inc., New York.

www.crownpublishing.com
www.tricyclepress.com

Tricycle Press and the Tricycle Press
colophon are registered trademarks
of Random House, Inc.

Library of Congress Cataloging-in-Publication Data

Long, Ethan.
  Bird and Birdie in a fine day / Ethan Long. — 1st ed.
    p. cm.
  Summary: Bird and Birdie enjoy a beautiful
morning, a wonderful afternoon, and a marvelous
evening together.

[1. Birds—Fiction. 2. Day—Fiction.] I. Title.
PZ7.L8453Bir 2010
  [E]—dc22
              2009022221

ISBN: 978-1-58246-321-6

Printed in Singapore

Design by Tasha Hall
Typeset in Birdlegs and Aged
The illustrations in this book were
rendered in Photoshop.

1 2 3 4 5 6 — 15 14 13 12 11 10

First Edition

For Kim P., who flew back into my life one day.-E.L.

I'm GREAT!
Isn't it a beautiful morning?
Yes, it IS
a beautiful morning!

STORY 2

A Wonderful AFTERNOON

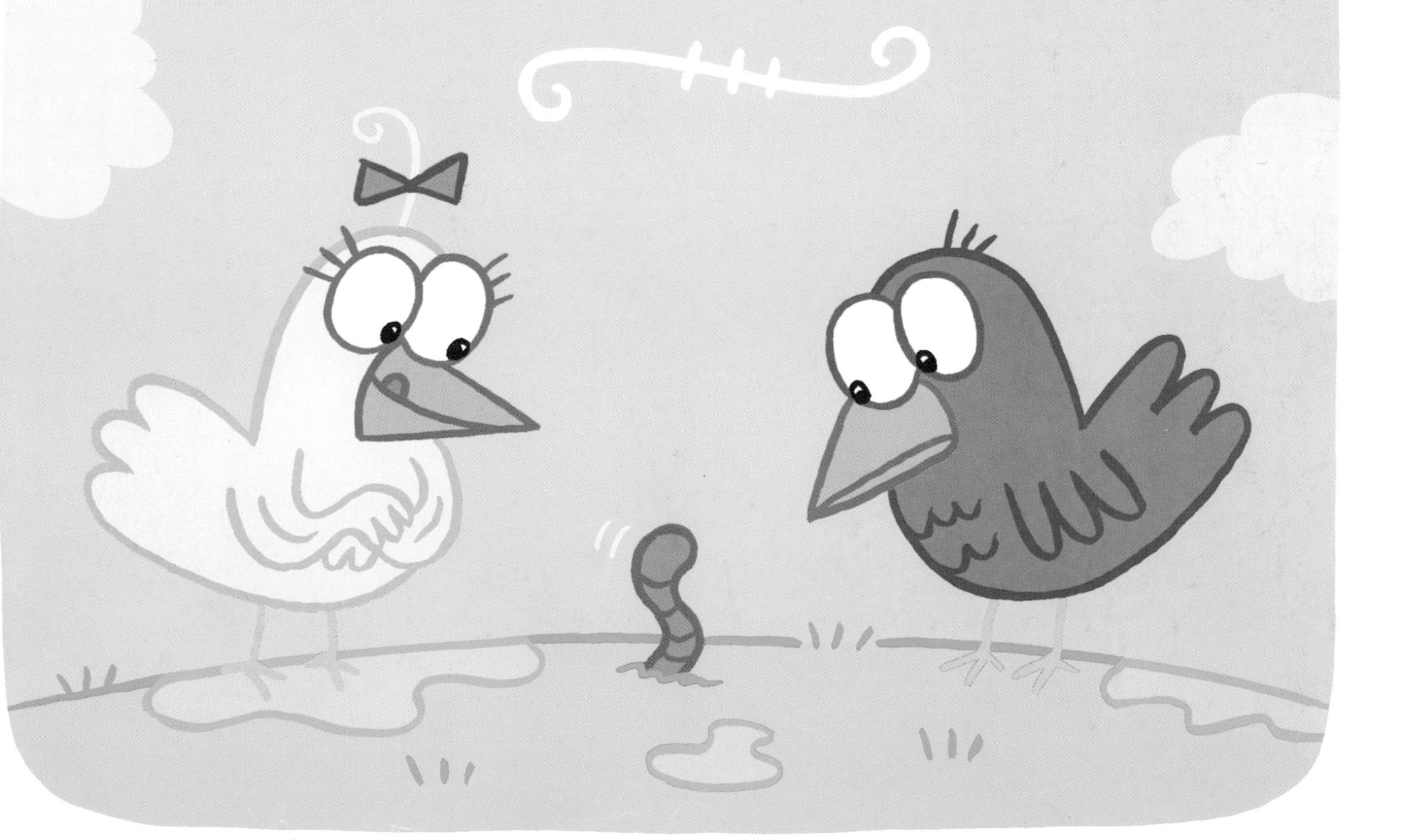

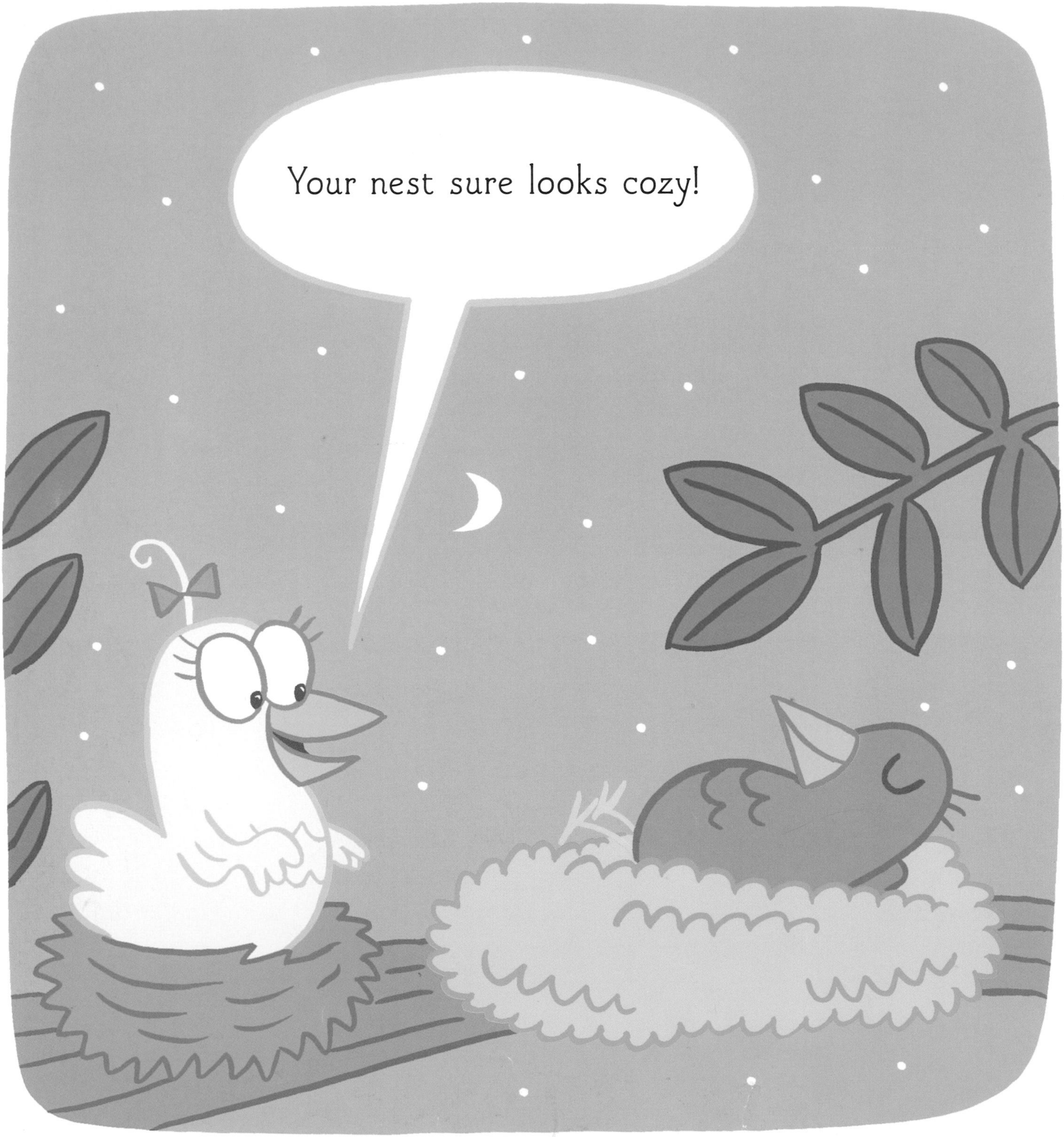
Your nest sure looks cozy!